The Sensitive Pirate

Written and illustrated by
Morgan W. Richie

For the kids in my life.
And for the adult kids, too.

Acknowledgements

Thank you to Sarah A. Younger and Alex Ho for being supportive and encouraging me throughout my process. I would also like to thank Cynthia Derosier who convinced me that I could do my own illustrations, Coree Carver who coached me on marketing, Melanie Hanns for proofreading, Cai Jiayin for translating the poem into Mandarin characters for a future edition, Dr. Kevin Lee Fujimoto for writing the connections questions, and Jean Higgins for creating a custom muffin recipe.

I would like to give a big hug to my beta-readers who provided important feedback. Thank you to Kathryn Antman, Ian Antman, Bonnie Becker, Mira Selkin, Solly Selkin, Amanda Barraza, Daisy Barraza, Lilibelle Barraza, Erin Bowen, Collin Bowen, Gabrielle Crowe, Grayson Crowe, Dane Crowe, Everly Crowe, Lianne Deren, Aliza Deren, Chase Deren, Molly Hayden, Oscar Blu Buddemeier, Jennifer Long, Jacob Long, Kinsley Long, Loren McClenachan, Sonora Neal, Osian Neal, Bob Meese, Charlotte Meese, Scout Meese, Priya Lalwani Purswaney, Neha Purswaney, Ashish Purswaney, Prabha Jethwani, Samarth Jethwani, Bani Jethwani, Cari Salkin and her classes, and Julia, Luke, and Malia.

For all of the people I've met who are learning who they are and are brave enough to become their best, authentic selves, thank you for the inspiration.

You be You.

On the blue and sparkling seas
Atop great waves and in the breeze
Sailed a pirate on a ship
Sword slung low on his hip.

The pirate seemed a hardened soul
Who ate live crabs from a bowl
And spent his nights in the gloom
Down in the ship's dark bedroom.

This pirate had a name, he did,
But no one said it, they just hid.
All adults would step aside
And boys and girls would run inside.

Rupert was this pirate's name
And at the height of his fame
Was dreaded greatly across the sea
As terrible as a pirate could be.

Pirate Rupert would go out and plunder,
Surprise ships and take them under.
He'd steal their stuff and call it "booty"
Because that is a pirate's duty.

But some who knew him would confide
The Pirate Rupert had a softer side.
But surely his reputation would be done
If news got out that he was fun.

Late at night he'd start to thinkin'
That plunderin' was kinda stinkin',
And could he find a new way to be
When all he knew was piracy?

In the dark of his cold abode,
His mind was heavy with a pirate's load
Of thoughts and worries floating by
And the secret that he was ... a nice guy.

But piracy was all he knew!
What other jobs could a pirate do?
He liked people, but he feared
They would think that he was weird.

Then one day it came to pass
That on a ship there was a lass,
Six years old and super smart
With freckles and a very kind heart.

Her name was Sarah, but they called her Sunny
And she liked people who were funny.
She'd heard of pirates in storybooks
And of their travels and exotic looks.

Rupert boarded the ship with a powerful yell
He saw Sunny and then he fell
Upon the deck in a great big splat
And in a flurry lost his hat.

Oh no! He thought, "What a chore!
I'm hardly scary on the floor!"
He leapt to his feet and almost cried
When he saw Sunny by his side.

Sunny looked at him with smiling eyes
And then she laughed, to his surprise!
She thought he was funny, yes she did,
And now it was he that ran and hid.

But it's funny how things can be
As he peered around the mast and she
Smiled a smile meant for him
And his heart swelled up and he fell again.

More laughter came from the child
And the pirate thought, "This is wild!
It's fun to make a person giggle,
I wonder what will happen if I wiggle?"

Then Pirate Rupert, forgetting his place,
Wiggled his nose and made a face.
But suddenly he looked around
And saw many faces peering down.

At first the faces were so stern
He felt his ears begin to burn.
"Oh great" he thought, "my secret's out!"
But no pirate should ever pout.

So the Pirate Rupert took a chance
And broke into a silly dance!
He crossed his eyes and shook his bum
And gave the little girl a plum!

Then the smiles began to spread
And a new thought entered his head.
"I love muffins and telling jokes,
And people seem to be nice folks."

"For a pirate, I'm pretty funny.
I wonder if I could make some money
Raiding ships and then not taking,
But leaving laughs and perhaps some baking?"

The Pirate Rupert then discovered
That something good had been recovered.
"I'll be myself and trust that they
Will often like me anyway."

And so his thoughts began to spin
That true treasure comes from within.

The End

Connection Questions
by Dr. Kevin Lee Fujimoto

Spending time with your child is the best way to bond, helping also to develop their self-esteem and confidence. The time spent reading together not only improves their reading skills and assists with developing a greater understanding of the material, but it also offers a safe opportunity to share their thoughts and feelings.

Read the book through completely the 1st time to establish a flow through the complete story. Your child will be more receptive and enthusiastic to your inquiries with a greater knowledge of the entire narrative. Using open-ended questions will encourage a dialogue with your child. Some examples include:

Why do you think …?
What is happening …?
Why is the …?
What was your favorite moment in the story?
What happened? How did that make you feel?
What do you think the story was about?

Another suggestion is to relate aspects of the storyline that are similar to your child's experiences. Examples include:

What would happen if Pirate Rupert came to our house?
What would happen if Pirate Rupert tried to take our belongings?

Pirate Rupert is experiencing some internal conflicts such as feeling badly about his decisions (stealing from others) and peer pressure (not living up to expectations of being a good pirate). Open-ended questions will bring about a thought-provoking discussion with your child about these topics. Some suggestions include:

Why does Pirate Rupert take other people's things?
How do you feel about that?
How do you think those people felt who had their belongings stolen?
What were you thinking?
How has it affected him and those around him?
What is it about Pirate Rupert's situation that makes it difficult for him?
What happened that made Pirate Rupert start feeling different?
What do you think may happen if Pirate Rupert keeps stealing even though he knows it is wrong?
Have you ever felt this way?
How have you been coping with this problem so far?
Is there anyone who you think you can talk to about this?
Are you ok not knowing what to do? Are you ok making a mistake?
Have you ever made someone feel sad? Angry? Happy?
What happened? What did you do?
What have you done in the past to fix the situation?
What can be done this time to make things better?
What do you think will happen next?
Do you think Pirate Rupert will change his behavior?
If you were pirate, what kind of captain would you be?

Connection Questions continued

If you were Pirate Rupert's 1st mate, what might you do to help him?
What are some things you would say to him?

Your child is a unique individual with special qualities and characteristics. Listening to your child, knowing what is important to them, what their interests are, what brings them happiness, energy, and hope, instills a feeling that they are meaningful and important.

By providing positive affirmations and encouragement, your child will develop the courage to believe in themselves and that they are capable, talented, and valuable. By promoting and modeling perseverance, resilience, and integrity, children learn not only that it is ok to make a mistake but that they can learn, improve, and thrive from failure.

Encourage your child to believe in themselves and advocate for their own needs and rights while maintaining respect for others. Others may disagree, criticize, or judge them negatively. However, knowing that their differences are a strength and not a weakness, your child will develop a solid sense of individuality, confidence, and efficacy.

Write your own questions here.

Rupert's Muffins
Recipe by master muffin maker, Jean Higgins

Muffin Ingredients

Wet
1/2 cup butter (softened)
2 eggs
1/2 cup ginger beer
1/4 cup crushed pineapple (drained)

Dry
1/2 cup brown sugar
1/2 cup white sugar
1 & 3/4 cups all purpose flour
1 tbsp cinnamon
1/2 tsp ground cloves
1/4 tsp baking soda
1 & 1/4 tsp baking powder
Optional: 1/4 cup walnuts or pecans

Optional Crumble Topping Ingredients

1/4 cup butter (softened)

1/2 cup flour
1/4 tsp cinnamon
1/3 cup brown sugar

Instructions

Preheat the oven to 375 degrees. Mix the wet ingredients in a large mixing bowl. In a separate mixing bowl, mix the dry ingredients. Sift the dry indgredients into the wet ingredients and mix until smooth. Add 1/4 cup of your favorite nuts such as walnuts or pecans if you love nuts!

Add muffin cups to your muffin tin and spoon the batter into the cups until about 3/4 fu.

Make the optional crumble topping by mixing the dry ingredients together and then adding to the softened butter. Mix using a dough blender or potato masher until the mixture forms little balls.

Sprinkle the crumble topping onto the top of the unbaked batter. Bake for 20-25 mintues or until a toothpick is clean when inserted.

Draw and color your own pirate!
Add eyes, nose, mouth, arms, and clothes. Then color her or him!